KT-546-720

ROTHERHAM LIBRARY & INFORMATION SERVICE

This book must be returned by the date specified at the time of issue as the DUE DATE FOR RETURN
The loan may be extended (personally, by post, telephone or online) for a further period, if the book is not required by another reader, by quoting the barcode / author / title.

Enquiries: 01709 336774

www.rotherham.gov.uk/libraries

LONDON•SYDNEY

This story is based on the traditional fairy tale,
Chicken Licken, but with a new twist.
You can read the original story in
Must Know Stories. Can you make
up your own twist for the story?

Franklin Watts
First published in Great Britain in 2016
by the Watts Publishing Group

ISBN 978 1 4451 4788 8 (hbk)
ISBN 978 1 4451 4790 1 (pbk)
ISBN 978 1 4451 4789 5 (library ebook)

Series Editor: Melanie Palmer
Series Advisor: Catherine Glavina
Series Designer: Peter Scoulding
Cover Designer: Cathryn Gilbert

Printed in China

Franklin Watts
An imprint of
Hachette Children's Group
Part of The Watts Publishing Group
Carmelite House
50 Victoria Embankment
London EC4Y 0DZ

An Hachette UK Company
www.hachette.co.uk

www.franklinwatts.co.uk

MIX
Paper from
responsible sources
FSC® C104740
FSC
www.fsc.org

Chicken Tricken was clever, and
very good at tricks.

Tricks

4   99 Water Tricks

He loved tricking Ducky Lucky and Goosey Loosey.

Then one day some acorns fell.
"Look out, the sky is falling down!"
Chicken Tricken lied.
"Quick, follow me!" He led Ducky
Lucky and Goosey Loosey to a barn.

Then he flew back to the
farmyard, and ate up **ALL**
the corn by himself.

Chicken Tricken played this trick a lot. But he was soon bored of corn. "I want nicer dinners," he said. "And I want to do better tricks!"

So he flew out of the farmyard and into the woods.

There he met Little Red Riding Hood with a basket of iced buns. "Ooh, I'll trick her and get those!" thought Chicken Tricken.

"Look out, the wolf is coming,"
he squawked. "Quick, follow me!"

Little Red Riding Hood dropped her basket and followed him out of the woods, screaming.

Quick as he could, Chicken Tricken
flew back and ate all the buns.
"Yum, yum!" he clucked.

He came to a cottage. Goldilocks was inside eating porridge. "Time for another trick," he thought.

"Look out, the three bears are coming!" squawked Chicken Tricken. "Quick, follow me!"

Goldilocks followed him out of the wood, howling.

Chicken Tricken zoomed back to the cottage. He ate all the creamy porridge in the bowls. "Delicious," he clucked.

Next he came across a gingerbread house. Hansel and Gretel were nibbling the roof.

"Look out, the witch is coming!"
fibbed Chicken Tricken. "Quick,
follow me!"

Hansel and Gretel followed him out of the woods in a panic.

Chicken Tricken flew back and ate the **WHOLE** gingerbread house, all by himself.

Now his tummy was bursting.
He was too fat to fly so he lay
down for a rest ...

... but soon he was woken up by a furry nose sniffing him.

"Look out! The wolf, the three bears and the witch are coming!" barked the furry stranger.

"They're cross with you, because they can't find Little Red Riding Hood, Goldilocks, or Hansel and Gretel in the woods. Quick, follow me!"

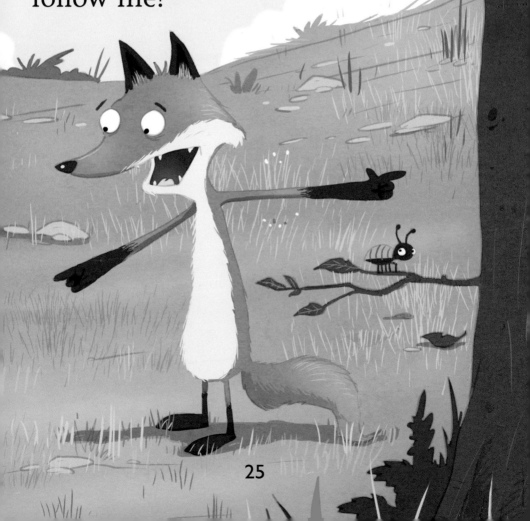

Chicken Tricken followed him. "Hide in this pie!" said the furry stranger.

MENU
Chicken
Chicken pie
Chicken pizza

Fat
Chicken
Pie

"Good idea," said Chicken Tricken, hopping inside. There he stayed...

...until he saw his chance to escape. He had TRICKED Foxy Loxy too!

Recipes for Chicken

Because Chicken Tricken really
was clever, and very good at tricks.

Puzzle 1

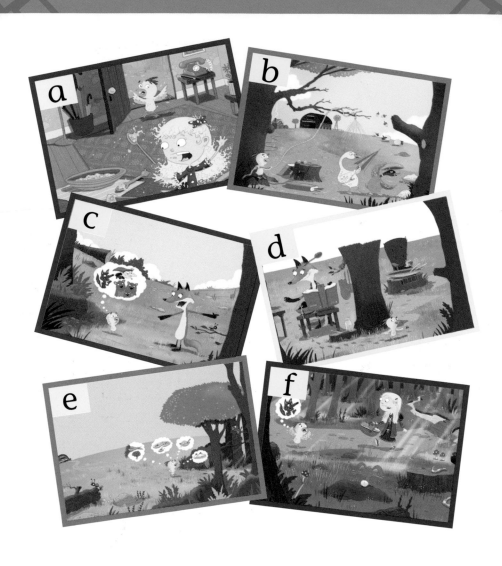

Put these pictures in the correct order.
Which event do you think is most important?
Now try writing the story in your own words!

Puzzle 2

Choose the correct speech bubbles for each character. Can you think of any others? Turn over to find the answers.

Answers

Puzzle 1

The correct order is: 1b, 2e, 3f, 4a, 5c, 6d

Puzzle 2

Chicken Tricken: 3, 5

Goosey Loosey: 2, 6

Foxy Loxy: 1, 4